What the experts* said al
novel, The Grea ... t

"I have never seen my children so engrossed in a book!"
**Heather Moorehouse**

"I couldn't put this book down! I ended up reading it in a day!"
**Ste Holmes**

"We laughed out loud but also had a lump in our throats."
**Jemma Morton**

"Cleverly written, with intrigue and a wonderful plot."
**Lucie Hutson**

"The writing is full of heart and humour. A wonderful book!"
**Ceri Looker**

"All ages can enjoy this funny story. Amazing!"
**Leanne Albon**

*Amazon Reviewers

# Books by Daniel Henshaw

*The Great Snail Robbery*
*The Curious Case of the Missing Orangutan*
*Jeremy's Shorts*

# JEREMY'S SHORTS

## DANIEL HENSHAW

First published 2019

ISBN 9781093283631

Cover artwork and illustrations by Jimmy Rogers
booyeah.co.uk
Twitter: @jimmyrogers

For Grandad John,
who taught me to
"tek it steady."

To Hugo
Happy reading!

# CONTENTS

# YOU'VE GOT SNAILS

I woke to the sound of screaming.

*Again.*

Coming through the walls from next door.

Dad had mentioned sound-proofing my room but he'd never gotten round to it. Then he'd left us to move in with his new girlfriend. So now I was stuck with our neighbour's high-pitched wailing.

The screams weren't coming from a baby, or a girl, or a distressed damsel on TV. No. It was a ten-year-old weirdo named Sanjiv.

Sanjiv may have been the same age as me – but he was nothing like me. He had long black hair and he never came out to play, not even on Saturdays. He went to a different school too and whenever he didn't get his own way, Sanjiv would scream the house down.

*"He's just a spoilt brat!"*

That's what Dad used to say. And Dad was right. I sometimes wondered if Sanjiv's screaming had been one of the reasons Dad left.

Rubbing sleep from my eyes, I climbed out of bed and crossed the room to my snail tank. Inside were thirty Giant African Land Snails. Yes, thirty. (I'd recently *'borrowed'* the pet snails from school. When I returned them, I saw that they'd left me thirty little presents.) At the minute though, there was nothing 'giant' about them. Being less than a month old, they were no bigger than a pea.

"Morning gang," I said, peering into the tank. On the damp soil, I saw just five snails. They looked like tiny pebbles. The rest must have burrowed beneath the earth.

"Did you sleep well? Sorry about the noise. It's just Sanjiv next door. He's a spoilt brat. Hopefully he'll go out soon."

I hadn't named the snails yet. Other than their colours, they all looked very similar, so it was hard to think of any good names. And anyway, there were so many it would've been hard to keep track.

Trudging downstairs like a grumpy troll, I found Mum in the kitchen, fiddling with the vacuum cleaner.

"Sanjiv's screaming again," I announced.

Mum looked up, startled.

"Oh, Jeremy. Didn't expect you to be up this early."

"His screaming woke me. *Again.*"

Mum didn't hear me. Or pretended not to. She moved the vacuum cleaner to one side.

"Jeremy, we need to talk."

"Didn't you hear what I said? That brat next door –"

"Don't call him that," Mum snapped. "Sanjiv has… *problems.*"

Tutting, I opened the cereal cupboard. "We've all got problems, Mum. I spent last night doing maths homework *and* I've got a spelling test on Monday and… great, we're out of Coco Pops! Maybe I should start screaming like Sanjiv."

"That's enough!" Mum stormed angrily to the kettle. She filled it with water, before clicking it on. "I don't want to hear any more about Sanjiv, Jeremy. We need to talk about your snails."

This took me by surprise. "What about my snails?" I grabbed a banana from the fruit bowl.

"Well…" Mum shifted awkwardly from one foot to the other. "We need to get rid of some."

I peeled the banana. "Get rid of some what?"

"Get rid of some snails."

My heart skipped. "What? Why?" I said this with a mouthful of banana, so it actually came out as, "Bop? Bye?"

"We don't have room for thirty snails, Jeremy."

Steam rose from the kettle before it clicked. Mum poured hot water into our mugs.

"But they're tiny," I said. "Like bits of sweetcorn."

"You know they won't stay that size, Jeremy. You've got those two at school. They're massive! And I saw one on the YouTube that was bigger than Stan."

Stan was my cousin Floyd's pet rabbit. It had terrifying red eyes so Floyd wanted to name it Satan, after the devil. Luckily, my cousin can't spell, so he wrote Stan on the form at the rescue centre.

"Yeah but –"

"You can keep six," said Mum, stirring the tea bags. "That's plenty."

I sighed before attempting to haggle.

"Ten," I suggested.

"Six," Mum replied.

"Nine."

"Six."

"Eight."

"Six."

It wasn't going well.

"Seven," I said. "Come on, Mum. Please. Lucky Seven."

She huffed, opening the fridge for milk. "Fine. You can keep seven."

I punched the air with delight… despite the fact that I'd just lost twenty-three of my pet snails.


Two hours later, just as I'd picked out seven snails to keep, Mum entered my room. She practically had the words *BAD NEWS* carved across her forehead.

"Jeremy, I've just spoken to Mr Letchkov."

Hearing that name made me shudder. I had a patchy history with Mr Letchkov, the owner of our local pet shop. Earlier that year, he'd tricked me into paying for some broken crocodile eggs. (But that's a different story entirely.)

"He doesn't want any snails." Mum paused, taking a deep breath. "He says the best thing to do… is, erm…"

"What?"

"He says we should, erm, put them in the freezer."

This time I frowned. "Why would we put them in the freezer? That's stupid."

Mum's eyes shifted around the room. "Mr Letchkov says, erm, that it's the… best way to, erm…"

"To *what?*"

Mum sighed. "It's the best way to kill them."

My lip began to quiver. "Kill them? You can't kill them! That's murder!"

"It's the most humane way to do it," said Mum softly, sitting down on my bed.

"Humane? There's nothing humane about it. It's murder! It's… it's…" I racked my brain for death-related words. "It's manslaughter. It's snail-slaughter!"

Mum shook her head. "Mr Letchkov says you just put them in the freezer and they go to sleep. They won't feel a thing."

"No way," I said, turning my back on Mum and storming over to the window. Sanjiv was now in next door's garden, his hands pressed into the soil like he was making a sandcastle... or a soil-castle. Such a weirdo.

"You can't freeze them, Mum. It's not fair. Somebody must want them."

"Well, I'm sorry Jeremy but I'm too busy to find anyone."

Behind me, I heard Mum get up off the bed and walk over to me. She placed her hands lightly on my shoulders, before kissing the top of my head.

"What's Sanjiv doing?" she asked.

"No idea. I don't care as long as he's quiet."

We stood in silence, watching our strange, long-haired neighbour playing in the dirt.

"How about this then," Mum eventually said. "How about *you* try to find someone who wants the snails? We can wait until next Saturday, before the snails start growing too big. That'll give you a whole week to find them a new home."

*A whole week.* As soon as Mum said it, I could feel the seconds ticking by. I turned away from the window, looking up at Mum.

"But what if I don't find anyone by next Saturday?"

She gave me a sad smile. "Then they'll have to go in the freezer… before they get too big."

*A whole week.*


I started immediately, making a poster with my best stencils and felt tips. I drew a huge picture of a snail in the middle, writing the details in bold.

### 23 Giant African Land Snails.
### FREE to a good home.
### Grow 8 inches long.
### Love cucumber and lettis.
### Call Jeremy.

I added Mum's mobile number to the bottom.

Because I did everything so carefully, the poster took me over an hour to make. It looked awesome. Mum was impressed too, even though I'd spelled *lettuce* wrong.

"Where shall I put it?" I asked her.

Mum arched an eyebrow. "You're only making one?"

I looked down at my masterpiece. "It took ages. I can't waste any more time. I need to get the word out before next Saturday."

"Take it to *Stones*," said Mum. "Get some photocopies."

Half an hour later, I marched out of *Stones Mini Market*, armed with twenty A3 copies of my poster. The shop's owner, Peter Stone, even let me put one near the entrance. Everyone would see it.

On the way to the store, I'd been to call for my best friend, Michael, and he'd agreed to help.

"Don't you want them?" I asked him, as we strode into town. "Maybe not all of them, just a few?"

Michael shook his head. "Nah. I'm allergic to anything with a shell. I can't eat prawn or crab. I'm terrified of turtles. And I collapsed once in a petrol station 'cause there was a big shell on the sign outside."

I nodded but didn't say anything.

"Where are we going first?" Michael asked. "We need to find the prime locations, the best spots. I've done this sort of thing before when I worked for a nightclub in London."

"Wherever," I shrugged. The truth: Michael had never worked for a nightclub in London. In fact, I don't think he'd even *been* to London. But he always told little stories like this to make his life sound more exciting. I just went along with it, never bothering to challenge him anymore.

Now, you'd think that giving away exotic pets would be easy, wouldn't you? It isn't. No other shopkeepers were as welcoming as Peter Stone. In fact, not a single shop would display my poster.

*"Snails? Why would anyone want snails?"*

*"That poster's too big for our noticeboard."*

*"Sorry, it's against our policy to advertise anything."*

*"It's fifty quid to put up posters in here."*

*"This is a garden centre. Snails are the gardener's nemesis."*

*"This is a pub. Get out."*

After we'd been rejected from Radiator World because our poster wasn't relevant to heated water systems, I wanted to give up. With just one poster on display, I felt totally deflated.

"Why don't we try *Eye Carumba*, the opticians?" I suggested.

Michael shook his head. "You need prime locations. No one ever goes in *that* opticians. And those who do can't see anyway."

Then, as we were passing St Mary's Church, Michael had a sudden brainwave.

"When I worked for that London nightclub," he said, "we put posters up wherever we could. Random places, without asking for permission. It's called Guerilla Advertising."

"Gorilla advertising?" I said. "What do gorillas have to do with advertising?"

Michael shrugged. "I don't know but that's what it's called. Maybe it's because gorillas can climb up high and stick posters where nobody else can reach."

"Yeah, you're probably right."

"Why don't we split up, put posters around town, and meet back here in an hour. You need to get them into prime locations, places that everyone will see."

We parted ways and I began searching. It was hard because all the shopkeepers had said we couldn't put posters *inside* their shops, and that probably meant *outside* too.

I walked around aimlessly for fifteen minutes before eventually spotting somewhere. Just down from the marketplace, a sign outside a house had changed from *'For Sale'* to *'Sold'*.

*Well,* I thought, *if it's been sold, they don't need to advertise it.*

Happy I was doing the right thing, I climbed onto their garden wall, sticking a poster over the 'Sold' sign.

After that, I saw the post box. People posted letters all the time and there was no shopkeeper to say I couldn't put it there. So I did. Then I stuck one on a bus stop. And then a litter bin in the middle of town. This was easy.

*Gorilla advertising.*

I stuck one on an oak tree, one on a bench, and two on the walls near the train station. I was just attaching my ninth poster to a telephone box, when a voice behind me sent a chill through my bones.

"You do know that's illegal, don't you?"

Jade Jackson had long brown hair and thick red lips. She wore way too much perfume, took way too long in the shower and was an awful cook. How did I know this? Because Jade

Jackson was my dad's new girlfriend, the woman he'd left Mum for.

The worst thing about her catching me with the poster, however... she was a police officer.

Turning to face her, I didn't answer. Jade stood with another officer, a man, both kitted out in black and white uniforms.

"Do you know it's illegal, Jeremy?" she asked.

I shrugged, not wanting to talk to her.

"Well, it is," she went on. "You're not allowed to just put posters up anywhere. We've seen them all over town."

My heart suddenly skipped as the number twenty-three bus chugged by... with a snail poster attached to its rear end... which was weird because I'd not put one on a bus.

Jade was still talking. "You've even got your name on them, Jeremy, and your mum's phone—"

"Don't talk about my mum!"

"Hey!" said the male officer, moving in front of Jade and invading my personal space. His voice was deep and stern. "Relax. We're just trying to help before you get in trouble. If people see these all over town and report you, you could get taken to court and be forced to pay a big fine. Do you have enough money to pay a big fine?"

"I have seven pounds and forty three pence in my piggy bank."

The policeman smiled. "I don't think that would be enough."

"Look, Jeremy," said Jade, "all we're asking is that you take down the posters and then it's not a problem."

The man brushed past me and grabbed the poster from the telephone box. "What are they anyway?" he asked, looking my sheet of A3 up and down.

"I'm trying to re-home my snails. If they don't find a new home before Saturday, Mum is going to freeze them and they'll die."

"What?" said Jade. "Why's she going to do that?"

"Because killing baby snails is nicer than stealing someone's husband!"

The policeman placed a hand on my chest. "Hey, calm down, fella. Look, you're obviously trying to do something good here but you can't just stick posters up wherever you like. You need permission. So, you either get permission or you take the posters down. Okay?"

I nodded, scowled and then sulked as I retreated around town, collecting my gorilla advertising campaign. By the time I'd removed the last of my posters, it was time to meet Michael.

Another hour had flashed by and I'd achieved absolutely nothing.

A swarm of dark clouds gathered above us as we sat on a bench near the church.

"How did it go?" I asked, before releasing a huge yawn.

"Woah! You a bit tired, mate?"

I shook my head. "I'm okay. Just had an early morning. Sanjiv from next door woke me up. He was screaming at the crack of dawn."

Michael tutted. "Must be scary living next to him. You hear that he bit a teacher at the special school?"

"He's nuts. I don't really see him much though, thank God."

Wincing, I glanced around the churchyard, hoping that nobody had heard me blaspheme. Luckily, there were no other people around and, other than the birds chirping happily in a nearby tree, all was quiet. Thank God. I told Michael about that ugly moose, Jade Jackson, and was just telling him that I wanted to give up, when my eye caught on something in the graveyard.

"What the heck is that?" I asked, jumping up from the bench.

Michael grinned. "Now *that* is what I'm talking about. Guerilla advertising."

I marched into the cemetery. "You can't put a poster on someone's gravestone!"

"Why not?" said Michael. "He's hardly going to complain, is he? It's the grave of Alfred Tomlinson. He was the oldest man in the country when he died. One hundred and twelve. That headstone's a tourist attraction."

"Exactly!" I said, staring at the poster in disbelief. "You can't put it there."

"People come to see this grave. It's a prime location to advertise."

"It's disrespectful."

"It's creative. Alfred would've loved it."

"How on earth do you know? And I saw one on the back of the number twenty three bus!"

Michael beamed. "That was my favourite. Anyone driving behind will see it."

"Yes, but it'll get me in trouble. Just like this one."

I was about to rip the poster off the headstone when I noticed a dark shape out the corner of my eye. A tickle of fear ran down my neck as I realised that we were being watched. A tall figure stood by the church's oak-panelled doors.

Now, when you think of a vicar, you would probably imagine a friendly man or woman who says kind things about everyone, even about horrid people like Braydon Spitz who once squirted vinegar in Michael's hair during a school trip to the pantomime, making him stink for the entire day while I sat next to him.

Vicars usually help people through tough times and say reassuring phrases like *'God works in mysterious ways'* or *'Follow the path of Jesus',* neither of which are particularly helpful because when *'God works in mysterious ways',* he lets horrible things happen like hurricanes and traffic jams and commercial breaks in the middle of your favourite cartoon. And it's practically impossible to *'Follow the path of Jesus'* because Jesus lived 2000 years ago in Jerusalem and life would have been very different back then because they didn't have cars or YouTube or Mario Kart, so it's difficult to know how Jesus would have behaved these days.

Anyway, vicars are usually nice people. But Reverend Partridge was a different matter entirely. The tall, thin vicar with his pale, skeletal face watched us from the church doors through two dark eyes that were sunk deep into his skull. He wore a long black robe that draped all the way down to his shins, giving him the appearance of a raven, the symbol of death.

"This is not an amusement park," he hissed, his voice slithering through the graveyard like the ghost of a snake. "What are you boys doing?"

Quick as a flash, I snatched the poster from the headstone.

Reverend Partridge terrified me. I once heard him tell somebody that if she did not follow the Ten Commandments of the Bible then she would end up burning in Hell for eternity and be tortured by the devil every morning and she would never be allowed cereal or toast for breakfast. And that person was a four-year-old girl named Isla Corrigan and it made her cry.

But before I'd thought how to avoid Reverend Partridge, Michael was already strutting towards him. I had no option but to follow.

"We need to ask you something," said Michael, the confidence in his voice matching his swagger.

Reverend Partridge showed us inside. The church's cool temperature hit me immediately. With its stone floors, high ceilings and thin windows, the church was like walking into a fridge.

We stood near the entrance. Rows of pews led to the front. To our left was a seating area with bookshelves filled with Bibles and a table covered in crayons and colouring books. The thing that caught my eye, however, was the community noticeboard, advertising a charity bake sale, a missing pensioner and a nursery school's production of Hamlet. The perfect place for a snail poster.

Other than us and Reverend Partridge, there was nobody else inside.

"Yes?" hissed the vicar, his voice echoing around the empty church. "Make this quick. I have things to do." Up close, he was even scarier than I'd remembered, with his cold, pale eyes and his thin, grey lips.

"Well," said Michael, "we're looking for places to hang some posters. We want to give these snails away before Jeremy's mum freezes them to death."

The vicar's eyes narrowed as Michael handed him a poster. He spent a few seconds reading the information before making his decision.

"No."

"What do you mean, no?" I asked, speaking for the first time.

Reverend Partridge looked at me like a giant germ who'd been sent by the devil.

"No. You can't put a poster up."

"But… but you have other posters," I said, pointing at the noticeboard.

"Yes," said the vicar. "And if you look more closely, you'll see that none of them advertise snails or slugs or bugs. I detest those horrid creatures and I refuse to place that poster on our noticeboard."

We stood in a deathly silence for a moment, Reverend Partridge's cold eyes watching us like a vulture. I think he was about to ask us to leave when Michael played a trump card.

"But isn't there something in the Bible about God loving all animals?" he said, secretly elbow-bumping me afterwards (it was our alternative to a fist-bump or a secret handshake).

The vicar sighed. *"The Lord is good to all; He has compassion for all he made.* Psalm 145."

"And there was Noah's Ark," I added. "Didn't God ask Noah to save *every* animal? That would've included Giant African Land Snails."

"Yes," said Reverend Partridge. "I know all about the Bible, thank you very much. And, yes, God may love every creature on this planet. Unfortunately, however, *I* do not. So take your posters elsewhere. They are *not* going on my noticeboard. Goodbye, gentlemen."

With that, he marched off to the other side of the church, leaving us to make our own way out.

As I was turning to leave, though, Michael grabbed my arm and silently shook his head. We watched the vicar disappear into a room elsewhere. Then Michael came to life.

"Give me a poster," he said.

I frowned. "But we're not allowed."

Michael grinned. "He said we can't put one on the noticeboard. But he didn't say anything about putting one on there." He pointed to the front of the church, snatched a poster from my hand and marched down the aisle between the pews.

"Where?" I asked, chasing after him.

"There.  On the DJ booth."

I looked to where he was pointing.  "You mean the pulpit?"

"Yeah, whatever.  Guerilla advertising.  Remember? Everyone in church looks up there so they'll all see the advert. If Reverend Partridge doesn't notice, it'll be there for the service tomorrow.  Sometimes you have to take a chance, Jez. Your snails' lives depend on it."

Michael did have a point.  Tomorrow was Sunday.  Half the town would see my poster if we secured it to the pulpit.

Michael pulled the blu-tac from his pocket and started sticking my advert to the front panel.  Knots twisted in my stomach. Was this really a good idea?  Mum's phone number was on there too.

"Are you sure about this?" I whispered.  "Isn't this, like, against God or something?"

"Pah," coughed Michael.  "God loves all animals, remember? He wants your snails to live, not to be iced to death in a freezer next to the Soleros."

After placing four blobs of blu-tac onto the pulpit, he pressed the poster into place.  We took a step back to admire his work.  I had to give Michael some credit. If a church full of people saw this, I'd re-home the snails in no time.

But then we heard the voice.

"Good God!" The vicar's exclamation boomed through the church like a clap of thunder. "What in the name of Jesus do you think you're doing?" We turned around to see Reverend Partridge standing at the end of the aisle like a dark shadow.

Michael frowned. "Are vicars meant to talk like that?"

My heart pounded. "I don't know. But I think we should run."

So we did. We darted between the pews, heading for the exit. Annoyingly, the vicar read our thoughts and ran in the same direction, his black cloak trailing behind him like a second-hand Batman cape.

We arrived at the oak doors just as the vicar stepped before them, blocking our way. I was about to turn and find another exit but Michael didn't slow down at all. He slid feet-first – like a footballer's slide-tackle – beneath the vicar's cloak and between his legs, disappearing through the open door of the church.

I attempted to do the same. Unfortunately, I wasn't as sporty as Michael. In fact, I was terrible at football. I played for the school team once and was awarded Player-of-the-Match… for the opposition.

As I slid across the floor, it wasn't until I was right near the vicar that I realised I'd misjudged it. Rather than going between his legs, I headed directly towards his left shin. I closed my eyes, bracing, before crashing into his leg, sending him tumbling to the ground beside me, his cloak draping me in darkness.

I felt sick. I could barely breathe. I'd just done a two-footed lunge on a man of God! That was a red-card offence in any ref's eyes.

I heard a terrifying growl beside me and expected to be grabbed by the ear and damned to Hell by the angriest vicar on the planet. But instead, I was yanked to my feet. The black cloak fell to the floor and daylight suddenly brought back my vision. Michael held me up, his eyes wide with fear. As he pulled me to leave, I looked down at the injured vicar. Guilt churned in my tummy. He was writhing around on the floor worse than a diving Brazilian winger. I couldn't just leave him there.

"Reverend Partridge, I'm so sorr–"

"Get out!" he shrieked. "Leave this church and don't ever come back!"

Michael tugged my arm again and this time I went with him. We ran. We ran and ran until we finally arrived back at my house, both dripping with sweat.

And only then did I realise I'd left the poster on the pulpit... with my name on it... and Mum's phone number. I think I needed to say a prayer.


Before parting ways, Michael and I decided that if Reverend Partridge phoned my mum, we'd both deny going to church. We concocted a story that some older lads stole my posters and must have stuck them around town. I didn't want to lie to Mum but none of this would've happened if the vicar had just been friendly. That's what we told ourselves anyway.

Closing the front door gently, I crept up to my room before flopping into my desk chair. I looked at the comic book on my desk. I'd created it with Michael.

*The Awesome Adventures of Jeremy Jaguar and Michael Mandrill*

The characters were basically us two but whenever trouble brewed in the world, we changed into our superhero alter-egos. Jeremy Jaguar had large claws to attack his enemies. Michael said he was a Wolverine rip-off, so I gave him some pointy teeth too.

Michael's character was a mandrill, one of the monkeys with the blue and red faces. His special power was the ability to jump really high and in our latest comic, Michael Mandrill needed this skill because a villain named Diesel McFreezle was trying to turn everyone to ice.

I was just adding a caption beneath Michael's drawing of Diesel McFreezle when an explosion of screaming erupted next door.

"I know it's not planned, Sanjiv," I heard Mrs Patel saying, "but we need to take these tablets to Betty."

More screams. A door slammed.

I wandered over to my window and saw Mrs Patel storm up the garden next door. She sat down on a bench with her head in her hands. Was she crying? I decided to go and cheer her up.

Mum didn't notice as I slipped out of the kitchen and into our garden. I peered over the fence at Mrs Patel. She looked exhausted. Exasperated. She jumped out of her skin when I spoke.

"Are you okay, Mrs Patel?"

She stared at me with red eyes. "Oh, Jeremy. Hello. Yes, I'm fine, thanks."

"You don't look fine. Sorry. Is that offensive?"

She smiled, though she didn't look happy. "It's quite alright. I'm not offended. It's just been a… tough day. Well, a tough week."

"Would you like a felt-tip pen so you can draw on the top of my arm?"

Mrs Patel looked at me like I'd just done the most disgusting burp in human history.

"Excuse me?" she said. "A felt-tip pen? So I can draw on your arm?"

I nodded. "Yes. Then you'll have a *shoulder* to *cray-on*." I grinned. "Get it? A shoulder to *cray*-on, instead of '*cry* on'. It's a joke. I thought it might cheer you up."

Mrs Patel smiled, more warmly this time. "Thanks, Jeremy. And yes, I do get it."

A moment of silence passed by.

"Is there anything else I can help you with today?" I asked. "Seeing as you're having a tough week."

Mrs Patel shook her head. "No, it's okay. It's just Sanjiv. He gets terribly upset about things."

Dad's words, *'spoilt brat',* immediately jumped into my head, though I kept them to myself.

"Why does he get so upset?" I asked instead.

Mrs Patel sighed and looked away for a few seconds. "He has a condition called Asperger Syndrome. It means that his brain works differently to most other children, which is why he goes to a different school to you. In particular, Sanjv likes to have a very strict routine. That's why he's upset at the moment. I took Betty Wilkins to the hospital this morning. She's got a problem with her hip, you see. But she left her medication in my car. She's going to need it tonight, so I said we had to nip to Betty's house. She lives down by St Mary's Church."

The mention of this building made me tense. We still hadn't heard from Reverend Partridge about the slide tackle.

"But, of course," Mrs Patel continued, "going to Betty's house wasn't a part of Sanjiv's schedule today, which is why he's so upset."

I suddenly felt guilty, thinking of Sanjiv as a spoilt brat. Dad hadn't been right at all. Sanjiv had Asperger Syndrome, something I knew nothing about. Now I felt sorry for him... and Mrs Patel.

"How do you calm him down?" I asked.

Mrs Patel frowned. "We just have to give him time. He has a tent in his bedroom, where he goes for peace and quiet. Someone told us to get a pet once but it didn't work out. Dogs and cats are too unpredictable for Sanjiv. He couldn't cope. Guinea pigs were okay for a bit but the squeaking became too much for him. He couldn't stand it."

"I've been having problems with pets today too."

"Sometimes," said Mrs Patel, not listening, "Sanjiv likes to come into the garden to calm himself down. He digs his fingers into the soil. It seems to work somehow. He also likes finding slugs. He finds them quite relaxing. Probably because they're so slow. More predictable than cats, who just go off wherever they like, and dogs, who could start barking at any second. But don't worry, I always make him wash his hands when he comes back inside."

I nodded. "I always wash my hands after handling my snails."

Mrs Patel paused for a moment. "What do you mean?"

"The snails in my room. I wash my hands whenever I've picked them up."

"You have snails in your room?"

I nodded again. "Thirty. Giant African Land Snails. But Mum says I've got to get rid of twenty-three. I've been trying to give them away all day but nothing's worked."

Mrs Patel's eyes suddenly brightened. I could almost see the cogs turning in her brain. "Can I have a look at them?" she eventually asked. "The snails?"

I hesitated. "What for?"

"I'd just... I'd like to see them."

"Okay." Grabbing a brown bowl, I rushed up to my room and filled it with heaps of soil... and twenty-three snails. Mum, watching TV in the living room, never noticed me go back in. I cautiously carried the bowl back down the garden, where Mrs Patel remained. I reached over the fence, offering her the bowl. She took it from me, peering down at the soil.

"What's this?" she asked, wrinkling her nose.

"The snails," I replied.

Mrs Patel frowned. "I thought they were Giant African ones? Aren't they meant to be massive?"

"They will be. They're just babies at the minute. Look…" I reached over the fence and parted some soil until I found a snail with a yellow shell.

Mrs Patel gasped. "Oh, it's beautiful. Just a baby, you say?"

I nodded.

"Oh, Jeremy. These would be absolutely perfect. How much do you want for them?"

A flutter of nerves ran through my tummy. "What do you mean?"

"You said you were trying to get rid of them, didn't you? I'll buy them."

My palms became clammy as panicked thoughts flashed through my mind. Sanjiv's screams each morning. Michael's claims that he'd bitten a teacher. And what about this condition – Asperger Syndrome? Did that make him dangerous? What if he got upset and smashed one of the snails in? I couldn't bear the thought.

"They're not for sale," I announced.

Mrs Patel looked shocked. "But I thought you said –?"

"They're not for sale."

An awkward silence filled the air… until Mrs Patel broke it.

"Jeremy, I see what's going on."

"You do?"

"You're worried about Sanjiv."

I tried to keep my face neutral, neither agreeing nor disagreeing.

"You don't need to worry, Jeremy. Yes, Sanjiv gets upset. Yes, he screams the house down. Yes, he runs out to the garden to be alone. But it's all just sound and fury. He's all bark and no bite."

Mrs Patel passed the bowl of snails back over the fence to me.

"Jeremy, you've seen him through your window. The slugs, the soil, the snails. They're the things that calm him down. Twenty-three African Lands Snails would be perfect."

I glanced back at the house to see Mum now busy in the kitchen. She had no idea of the shady dealings taking place at the end of her garden.

"I tell you what, Jeremy. Why don't you bring the snails up to Sanjiv's room and see how he reacts. If you're not happy with how he treats them, take them back home. But if you think he might be okay with them… well… it's your decision."

I felt my knees wobble. Go to Sanjiv's room? Before today, I'd always assumed he was crazy. I would never have dared enter that house. But what was the alternative? Leave the snails unwanted? Allow Mum to chuck them in the freezer next to the ice cream? I had to take a chance… for the sake of those poor creatures.

Swallowing a big gulp of courage, I nodded at Mrs Patel.

"Okay, we can go and see him."

Mrs Patel grinned before walking to the very end of her garden, where the fence ended and a small wall stood low enough to be climbed over. I passed the bowl to Mrs Patel and then leapt over the wall into her garden.

We wandered into her kitchen, which smelled of cheap, oven-cooked food. I politely removed my trainers.

"We had fish fingers for tea," Mrs Patel announced. "Sanjiv likes food that can be kept separate from each other. The fish fingers can't touch the chips and the chips can't touch the peas."

We turned into the hallway. The carpets were colourful, with old-fashioned patterns throughout.

"I'll never get him to eat a curry," Mrs Patel added, a trace of sadness in her voice.

Once on the small landing, Sanjiv's room was the first door on the left. Mrs Patel knocked lightly before turning the handle and gingerly pushing her way inside. The room was dark, the curtains closed, the lights off.

Sanjiv had two posters on his wall. One displayed constellations of stars: Orion, The Big Dipper, Pisces the fish. I couldn't understand how people saw those images in a few stars but I guess they were clever Sciencey types, much smarter than me.

The second poster was titled *'The Periodic Table'*. It appeared to have loads of random letters scattered across it.

**Fe, Br, Au.**

I didn't really get it, though I did see some words I recognised.

**Oxygen, Silver, Iron.**

Like Mrs Patel had said earlier, Sanjiv had a yellow tent erected in his room, his place to chill out. But it wasn't until I glanced at the bed that my nerves tightened. There, lying on top of the duvet with a Kindle lighting up his face, was the long-haired boy who filled my heart with fear.

Were we interrupting his schedule? This was an unplanned visit. What if he attacked me? Bit me, like his teacher!

"Sanjiv?" Mrs Patel spoke softly. "Can I talk to you for a while?"

This was followed by a long, long… looooooong silence, before Sanjiv eventually lifted his head from the bright, white light of the Kindle.

"Yes?" He seemed surprised to see me, frowning deeply, and I immediately felt this was a mistake.

"Jeremy's come around from next door. He's brought you a present."

Sanjiv didn't look at me. He kept his gaze on his mother, practically scowling.

Another lengthy pause.

"What present?"

"Well, you know how you like playing with the slugs in the garden?" Mrs Patel's soft voice has become sickly sweet, as if she were talking to a toddler. "Jeremy has some Giant African Snails."

Watching Sanjiv carefully, I noticed his face twitch. "*Land* Snails?" he said.

"Sorry?" Mrs Patel replied.

"Do you mean Giant African *Land* Snails?"

"Yes," I said, speaking for the first time.

Sanjiv's eyes darted to me before returning to his mum. "Can I look at them?"

This was the moment.

I had to decide whether I could trust this kid, who couldn't even make eye-contact, with the lives of my snails.

*He's all bark and no bite.*

But hadn't Michael told me he'd bitten a teacher?

Yes, but Michael once told me he'd flown to Venus with *Ryanair.* Michael once told me a pterodactyl flew over his garden, carrying an alligator in its mouth. Michael once told me that rabbits can lay eggs... if they try hard enough. Michael's word didn't mean too much.

*He's all bark and no bite.*

Mrs Patel wouldn't have said that unless she meant it. I decided to give Sanjiv a chance.

"Of course you can look at them," I said, placing the brown bowl on the floor next to the tent.

Sanjiv moved cautiously to the bowl before crouching and slowly pressing his hands into the soil. With his long, black hair hanging over his eyes, I couldn't see his facial expression. Then, seconds later, he pulled a snail from the dirt. Its shell was orange. When Sanjiv looked up, the moody face I'd only ever seen had been transformed. He was smiling... not only with his mouth but with two bright, white eyes.

"They're snails, Mum!" he said, still not looking at me. "Giant African Land Snails!"

There was an excitement in his voice that I'd never heard before and I watched as he delicately searched the soil for more snails. He picked them up and stroked them like they were soft kittens. I even heard him giggle. I'd never seen my neighbour so full of life.

When I glanced at Mrs Patel, I saw tears in her eyes... but not of sadness... not any longer. She looked my way. I nodded. I knew this was the right thing to do. Glancing once more at the snail bowl, I watched Sanjiv searching happily through the soil. As I began backing out of the room, I felt my heart flutter. I was about to leave when I remembered something important.

"You'll need a tank!"

"We have an old fish tank in the shed," Mr Patel answered. "Thank you so much, Jeremy."

"They like lettuce and cucumber best." My voice was beginning to crack. "And cuttlefish is good for their shells."

"Thank you, Jeremy. I'm sure Sanjiv will do plenty of research, won't you love?"

Sanjiv didn't answer. He was too busy with the snails. Smiling, giggling... and definitely not screaming.

I nodded once more at Mrs Patel and she showed me back downstairs. She thanked me again before I made my way home. I told Mum all about what I'd done and she seemed genuinely pleased... even proud of me. She said we could have my favourite pizza to celebrate and she was just about to order it when the phone rang.

"Hello?" she said into the receiver. "Oh, hello Reverend Partridge." As she listened to the phone, a dark frown clouded her face, before she glared right into my soul.

I had a feeling that she was going to change her mind about the pizza.

# JEREMY'S SHORTS

Okay, I admit it. I was acting like a pampered prince, demanding new shorts at the drop of a hat. But look at it from my point of view: I only had *one* pair of swimming trunks. And I mean *trunks*. When you get to the age of ten and a half, nobody wears trunks anymore. Everyone wears swimming *shorts*. Not trunks.

And today was the morning of the party; Yasmine Kumar's swimming party.

I demanded that Mum take me shopping. She moaned about being late for work and told me that we had to be quick.

"One shop, Jeremy. That's all."

Well, what a disaster! Most of the shorts were too small. The rest were too big. Only one pair fit me; some disgusting green ones, the colour of SNOT!

"They'll have to do," Mum said, pushing me towards the till. "Come on, or I'm going to be late."

"I don't want those!" I marched back to the rails of colourful swim shorts, grabbing the coolest pair I could see. "I want these." I held up a pair of orange ones with hundreds of little sharks on.

Mum sighed, still holding the snot shorts. "Jeremy, they're too big. Just have these, will you?"

"No! I want these!" Told you I was acting like a pampered prince.

Mum glanced at her watch before huffing.

"Fine! Have those. I suppose you'll grow into them. But, if they don't fit, don't say I didn't warn you. Remember that old saying, Jeremy: Mother knows best."

Snatching the orange shorts from me, she marched to the counter, paid her card and then hurried us out of the shop.

44

After Mum had rushed off to work, I met my best friend, Michael, and headed for our local swimming baths, *Aqua Adventures*. The August day was bright and hot, just the odd cloud in the sky. Birds sang in the trees, music blasted from passing cars and, as the time approached noon, beer gardens were already filled with loud, red-skinned women, who didn't appear to own any sun-cream.

"Did you get Yasmine a present?" Michael asked as we strolled along the main road.

I nodded. "Mum bought her a voucher for a clothes shop or something. Wasn't really paying attention. Did you?"

Michael nodded this time. "Got her a necklace. Four carat diamond." I didn't know this at the time but a four carat diamond necklace would be worth about £65,000. However, I *did* know that bending the truth was one of Michael's greatest talents in life, so there wouldn't be any real diamonds in the necklace.

Approaching the town centre, we waited at the crossing for the green man to come on before wandering across the main road.

"Did I tell you about the wave machine?" Michael asked. He meant the new contraption they'd installed at *Aqua Adventures*. A machine that created artificial waves, just like the real thing.

"I think you mentioned it," I said. Of course he'd mentioned it. Everyone had mentioned it. The installation of the wave machine was the most exciting thing to happen in our town since Neil Armstrong turned on the Christmas lights two years ago. Not until the actual night did we realise it wasn't *the* Neil Armstrong, seeing as the famous astronaut died in 2012. This was just some random bald bloke from Doncaster, who happened to have the same name.

Anyway, apparently, this new wave machine *was* the real deal. And yes, everyone had been banging on about it.

"It's *sooooo* good!" said Michael. "I went with my mum last week. An alarm sounds and then the waves start. They nearly touch the ceiling, launching people everywhere. I was actually thrown into the cafe and landed in someone's chips."

I laughed. This definitely *wasn't* true.

At *Aqua Adventures*, our classmates were by the entrance. Billy Kominski was there and Imogen Rutherford and, of course, Yasmine Kumar. The smell of chlorine hung in the air.

We handed over our presents and cards and said 'Happy Birthday'. Yasmine said 'Thanks' and gave me a fake smile. Once we'd all arrived, we made our way inside to the 'Changing Village'. The girls and mums went one way, boys the other.

Michael and I shared a changing cubicle, keeping ourselves private from the others.

"Nice shorts!" said Michael.

"Thanks," I replied. "Got 'em today. Brand new. They have sharks on."

"Very cool. Great White Sharks are my third favourite sea creature."

I nodded. "What are your top two?"

"Number two: Vampire Squid. They wrap their arms around themselves like they're wearing a cloak... like Dracula."

"Nice."

A picture of The Incredible Hulk stretched across the bum of Michael's shorts. He tightened them, pulling hard on the drawstring.

"And my number one," he said, "is a seahorse."

I arched an eyebrow. "A seahorse?"

Michael nodded enthusiastically. "Yeah. They're awesome. They're these tiny colourful horses that have long tails and can swim."

"Yes, I know what a seahorse is, Michael. You *do* know they're not actually horses though, don't you?"

"Erm, yeah." (I don't think he did.)

I tied my orange shorts as tight as they'd go (they were still a bit loose, but not too bad considering they were a size too big). We shoved our clothes into a locker and made our way poolside.

*Aqua Adventures* was a huge place with three pools, four slides and six water cannons dotted around the main pool. The hot, noisy atmosphere hit you as soon as you left the changing rooms, excitement echoing around the high ceiling. There was screaming and shouting, bombing and diving, somersaults and splashing. And that was just Michael.

I didn't really know the 'birthday girl' Yasmine Kumar too well because I wasn't really cool enough to be her friend. But everyone liked Michael, so I guess I'd been invited for being his mate. I was glad though. The party was great fun. The look on people's faces when you shot them with the water cannons was priceless. I only tried one water slide though; the water was so slow, I actually got stuck halfway down and had to drag my bottom along like a dog itching its bum on the carpet.

And then the hooter sounded. The wave machine was about to begin. Cheers bounced off the walls. Everyone charged to the pool.

The waves began slowly, gently pushing their way from the deep end to the shallows. The early ones did little more than rock us a bit and I thought Michael's description of the tidal wave that flung him into the cafe was just another tall tale.

But it soon changed.

The waves increased in size. The laughter increased in volume. Soon the water was throwing me in all directions. I lost Michael.

Then came the hooter again. The air filled with screams as the biggest wave I'd ever seen in my life came charging towards me like an enormous water monster, living only to destroy tiny humans. It flung me across the surface like a skimmed pebble, before swallowing me whole. I came up panting, laughing; my heart hammering a million beats per minute.

Michael had been right. The wave machine *was* cool and dangerous and… enthralling!

After the commotion had died down, I eventually spotted Michael and swam towards him in the deep end. We were both giggling when we found each other.

"That was sooooo good!" I yelled.

"Told you," said Michael. "My head hit the ceiling during the big one!"

We laughed some more before the joyful expression on Michael's face suddenly creased into a frown. His eyes narrowed as he peered at the water in front of us. His brown face seemed to pale.

"What's up?" I asked.

"Jeremy, you're…" He paused.

"What?"

He looked uncomfortable, glancing over each shoulder.

"Jeremy, you're, um, you're…"

My forehead crinkled in confusion. "What are you on about?"

"Your shorts. They're gone. You're… naked."

My eyes widened, my heart froze. My hands dunked beneath the water to feel where my shorts should have been. Nothing there but bare skin. The shorts must have come off during the waves! Anyone looking closely would be able to see my… *bits*.

Mum's words suddenly popped into my head.

*Mother knows best.*

Why hadn't I listened to her and just taken the snot shorts? Why hadn't I just stuck with my trunks?

My heart became heavy like a cold stone. My lungs tightened. My eyes flashed around the pool, searching for a floating clump of orange. *Aqua Adventures* was filled with colours; armbands, floats, inflatable flamingos. It was hard to see anything that resembled my shorts among the bodies and balls and splashing water.

"There!" Michael barked, pointing at the shallow end. "Right by the edge."

Relief washed through me as I saw my shorts floating next to a family with a toddler. The parents looked ready to leave.

Hopefully, I could grab my shorts and slip them back on without anyone noticing.

Thrashing our arms like windmills through the water, we attempted our best front crawl. I'd like to think we were going fast but we probably looked like a pair of sloths trying not to drown. I arrived in the shallow end first, as I'm a much faster swimmer than Michael – though he wouldn't agree (he claimed he'd once represented Ghana at the Junior Olympics).

Panting, my head flashed from side-to-side, looking for the shorts. But now I saw no sign of *anything* orange. With the water so shallow, I had to stay well below the surface so that nobody saw my… *nakedness*. I glanced around. The family with the toddler were gone too.

Michael arrived by my side, gulping huge breaths of air.

"Where are they?" he asked.

"I don't know. They've vanished!"

Michael pointed at the Changing Village. "There!"

I glanced round to see the toddler with his family. The little kid was holding my shorts in his hand, carrying them off like a favourite toy.

Michael looked at me. "What you gonna do?"

"ME?! I'm not going to do anything. In case you've forgotten, I'm literally wearing *nothing*! I'm risking it being in the shallow end."

Michael sighed. Didn't move.

"Go after him!" I yelled.

An expression of realisation exploded onto Michael's face. He splashed to the side of the pool and climbed out, before sprinting towards the Changing Village. A loud whistle immediately sounded.

"No running by the pool!" bellowed a huge female Lifeguard, who looked like she ate iron girders for breakfast. She was sitting poolside, on what looked like a massive high-chair for babies.

Michael slowed to a fast walk before disappearing into the Changing Village.

I swam back to the deep end and bobbed there for a while, treading water. My eyes constantly shifted, checking that nobody came too close.

"Come on, come on," I whispered, urging Michael to reappear.

What was taking him so long? The kid was only small. Surely it wouldn't take too much effort to take shorts off him.

Never mind. As long as I stayed away from every other person, I'd be okay.

"Hey, Jeremy," said Yasmine, the birthday girl. "What are you doing?"

The speed of my heartbeat tripled. I spun around in the water, immediately edging away from her. Yasmine was in the pool with Imogen Rutherford. They both wore proper bikinis rather than swimsuits, thinking they were grown-ups.

"Just waiting for Michael," I said, swimming slowly backwards. They both frowned, clearly noticing that I was moving away from them.

"Well," said Yasmine. "We're about to play Underwater Tag. Do you want to join us?"

"NO!" I yelled, far too quickly.

The girls flinched at my outburst, before raising their eyebrows.

"It's just," I said, "I, um, I need to find Michael. We're already playing a game."

"Oooh, can we play?"

"NO!"

More frowns.

"We, um, we can't have more than two players. It's, um, it's a game with very strict rules."

Without further explanation, I turned and swam away. I headed for the shallows but then remembered the lack of cover, so ended up doing a big loop of the pool, returning to the deep end. My heartbeat hadn't slowed. Could people see my bare body? Even in the deep end?

When I looked back at Yasmine and Imogen, they were fully invested in a game of Underwater Tag; splashing, laughing and trying to tag the others beneath the surface. They'd quickly forgotten that I was being a total weirdo. Thank goodness.

Then, glancing at the Changing Village, my heart skipped a beat. Michael appeared. But he didn't look happy. My guts twisted. His hands were empty. Where were my shorts?

He looked guilty as he slipped back into the water.

"What's going on?" I asked. "Where are my shorts?"

"The kid was with his mum," said Michael.

"And?"

"Well, he went into the *female* changing rooms. I can't go in there."

"What about the dad? Why didn't you ask the dad to get them?"

"I thought about that. But then realised I hadn't even looked at the dad. I didn't know which one he was."

I sighed, covering myself with one hand beneath the water.

"You'll have to go and wait outside the changing rooms."

"What? No way. I'm not getting out, drying myself, getting dressed and then standing out there, just to get changed all over again."

"Oh, well I'm sorry if that's going to spoil your afternoon, Michael, but in case you've forgotten, I don't have a single centimetre of clothing to cover myself."

Michael sighed. "It'll be too late now anyway. By the time I'm dressed, they'll be gone." He thought for a second before a lightbulb practically pinged above his head. "I know. I'll tell Yasmine. She can get the shorts for you."

"NO! Are you mad? You can't tell the girls. That would be as bad as getting out the pool and strolling around in the buff."

"Well, what else are we meant to do? I can't go in the women's changing rooms."

A plan quickly formed in my mind. Michael was right. He couldn't go into the female changing rooms but he *could* go into the male side. "I've got it. Go to our locker. Bring my boxer shorts. They'll just have to get wet."

"What about later?" Michael asked. "When we get out?"

"I'll have to go Pants-Free."

Michael climbed out of the water once more and sprinted along the side of the pool. The muscular lifeguard blew her whistle. She was going to tell him not to run again. She may have lectured him about the dangers of running near the pool.

But it was too late.

As Michael turned the corner, he slipped. His feet came from under him, smacking his head and elbow hard against the tiles! He came down with a BUMP! His thigh skidded across the hard surface, scraping his skin. The grimace on his face showed his pain.

The lifeguard leapt down from her high-chair before rushing to Michael. I wanted to help but couldn't leave the pool, obviously. Instead, I just watched as the muscular woman tended to my friend. She helped him to his feet and I breathed a sigh of relief.

But then she did something terrible.

The lifeguard began escorting Michael towards the First Aid room… in the opposite direction to the Changing Village! She opened the door and stepped inside with him. Another lifeguard took her place on the high-chair.

Now what? What was I supposed to do? I had no shorts on, no clothes at all, and the only person I could trust was injured.

I glanced around nervously. Paranoid. Every time someone looked my way, I panicked. Did they know? Could they see beneath the water? With every giggle I heard, I became convinced they were laughing at me.

Those words echoed at the back of my mind…

*Mother knows best.*

Yasmine and Imogen were no longer playing Underwater Tag. Everyone was doing their own thing now. And just as I was wondering how the heck I was going to get out of this situation, a boy from our class, Billy Kominski, swam by. Billy was the captain of the school football team and had bright blonde hair. A real cool guy. I decided to chance it.

"Billy," I hissed.

He turned to see where the sound came from.

"Oh, Jeremy. Thought you'd be with Michael. Did you see him fall?"

I nodded. "Listen, Billy. I need a massive favour."

He arched an eyebrow but didn't say anything.

"Could you please go to Michael in the First Aid room?" I pointed to where he'd been taken. "Get our locker key and fetch my boxer shorts from the changing rooms."

Billy glared at me like three noses had just appeared in the middle of my forehead.

"I'm not your slave, Jeremy. Go yourself."

He was about to swim away but I grabbed his shoulder. "I can't!"

"What do you mean?" asked Billy, narrowing his eyes.

"I can't get out of the pool. That's why I need you to go. Michael was getting my boxers when he slipped."

Billy frowned. "Why can't you get out of the pool? It's not cold."

I sighed. "I'm... You see, I, um... I've lost–"

"*What?*"

"My swimming shorts were too big for me and they came off. Now I've lost them. I'm naked."

My words seemed to register with Billy in slow motion. First his eyes widened in horror. Then his mouth slowly opened into a giant O. His nose crinkled in disgust... before his whole face brightened into a huge smile. Looking down at the water, he laughed so hard that snot snorted from his nose.

I smiled. "I know, pretty funny. So will you do it? Will you fetch my boxers for me?"

Billy snorted another uncontrollable laugh before turning and swimming away.

"Hey!" I yelled, but it was too late. He'd gone.

I watched him swim straight towards Yasmine and Imogen. He said something and pointed in my direction. The girls looked horrified but then laughed, covering their mouths with their hands. I remained in the deep end, treading water, as Billy and the others swam around, telling everyone about my predicament.

Within a minute or so, I sensed hundreds of eyes on me. It felt like the whole world was closing in around me. Nobody was interested in the water cannons any more, or the slides, or diving into the pool. Everyone wanted to see the naked boy in the deep end. They probably thought I'd done it on purpose. They probably thought I was a weirdo, a freak. I felt like an animal at the zoo, a strange creature for everyone to stare at.

With tears forming, I dipped beneath the water, curling into a ball and blowing out air. I quickly sank to the bottom, away from those eyes. Can you cry underwater? I wasn't sure. I felt safe for a moment but I knew it wouldn't last. There was only so long that I could hold my breath.

When I came back up, gasping for air, my eyes stung from chlorine. Wiping the water away, I gazed around the room before noticing, much to my horror, that Yasmine had pulled herself out of the pool and was walking towards the new lifeguard. What was she doing? She said something to the adult then pointed at me. I felt my cheeks burn.

Stepping down from her highchair, the lifeguard glared at me. What had Yasmine told her? The lifeguard lifted the whistle to her mouth and was about to blow it… when an alarm suddenly squealed, echoing around the high ceiling.

Horrified, I thought the wave machine was about to start again. I couldn't bear the idea of being thrown around the pool, butt-naked. Who knew where I'd get catapulted! I might land in someone's arms, nude as a new-born!

But this alarm wasn't the same as the one we'd heard before. More high-pitched, more urgent. Then the lifeguard did start blowing her whistle, but she was no longer looking at me.

"EVERYBODY OUT!" she yelled. "FIRE! THIS IS NOT A DRILL!"

Panic rippled through the air as people splashed to the edges of the pool, some screaming. What should I do? At first, I felt relieved about the distraction. Nobody cared about me anymore. But then it dawned on me: If there was a fire, I'd need to get out!

I heard a voice behind me.

"Jeremy!"

I spun around, still in the centre of the pool, while everyone else escaped. At the water's edge, I saw Michael, wide-eyed and edgy. He stood suspiciously close to a small red box attached to the wall.

"Hide!" he hissed, just audible above the alarm's wail. "Get under the water! Hide!"

Without hesitation, I swam to the now-deserted deep end, tucking myself into a corner. I glanced around the big room. Everybody was heading towards the exit, nobody looking my way. Taking a huge gulp of air, I pinched my nose before ducking beneath the surface, pushing myself right to the bottom of the pool.

The water muffled all the noise; the alarm and the chatter now deadened and dull. My lungs, full of air, squeezed tight against my ribs. As the seconds ticked by, my throat burned. I had to hold on a bit longer. My cheeks were puffed, my forehead tense. It felt like my chest might explode. I couldn't hold it anymore!

Soaring to the light above me, my face broke the surface of the water. I gasped for desperate breaths. I was making too much noise but I couldn't help it. Panting urgently, I needed air. Too noisy, much too noisy. I'd surely be caught now.

After a few seconds, when I'd eventually calmed my breathing, I looked around. I couldn't believe it. The place was empty. Checking over both shoulders, I gripped the edge of the pool and heaved myself out, dripping wet, everything on show.

I wouldn't be able to thank Michael enough. I just hoped he wouldn't be in trouble. Striding quickly by the side of the pool, a huge smile stretched across my face. Lucky, lucky boy.

Now I could deny it all. If the girls asked me about being naked in the pool, I'd just say that Billy was making it up. The girls would never know the truth.

Almost laughing, I turned the corner of the pool and headed towards the changing rooms. I pushed through the double doors with one hand covering my private area. It wouldn't matter too much if people saw me like this now... I was in a changing room after all.

But when I looked around the room, thirty bright eyes glared at my naked body... thirty female eyes. An explosion of shrieks and laughter filled the air as I realised... after everything... I'd walked into the girls' changing rooms by mistake.

Oh no! What had I done?

Those words echoed once more:

*Mother knows best.*

# SAVING PARROT BRIAN

Rain banged against the window like a million tiny drummers. We'd spent Saturday in my bedroom, making a comic book for our superhero alter-egos, Jeremy Jaguar and Michael Mandrill. Michael drew the illustrations while I added the captions. He was better at drawing and I could spell.

In our latest episode, the heroes were saving a friendly dragon that had been captured by an evil wizard.

"Why's your name always first?" asked Michael. "Jeremy Jaguar and Michael Mandrill. Why not the other way around? Michael Mandrill and Jeremy Jaguar."

I shrugged. "Just because."

"Because what?"

I shrugged again. "I write the words. I'm the author, so my name goes first."

"Surely the pictures are more important?"

I shrugged for a third time. "My name comes first. Alphabetically."

This seemed to satisfy him… for a moment.

"How come I'm only a monkey? You get to be a jaguar but I'm just a baboon."

My eyes narrowed. "Michael, you *chose* to be a mandrill."

"Only because you suggested it. I thought a mandrill was a power-tool. You know, a drill… for men."

I scratched my neck. "Well, you had to be something with an M. For alliteration. What would you have preferred? Michael Moth? Michael Moose? Michael Mole-Rat?"

My best friend shook his head. "It's just unfair. You're a jaguar, a predator. I'm a boring baboon."

"Boring? Mandrill's have a red and blue face! How is that boring? Plus, they have sharp teeth, they're good at climbing… and there's one in The Lion King."

Michael wandered over to my bedroom window, staring out at something. I joined him. The rain had stopped. Mr Mendoza

from number six was on his drive, wiping his wheelie bins.
Michael seemed lost in thought.

"You can change animals if you like," I said eventually. "But it'll mean a lot of changes to the comics."

Michael sighed, before saying: "Don't you ever get bored of just *making* superhero stories?"

"Not really," I said. "We've only made two. And they're only a page of A4."

Michael didn't hear me. "But what if we didn't just *write* about Michael Mandrill and Jeremy Jaguar. What if we *became* them?"

I arched an eyebrow. "What do you mean?"

"Superheroes exist because people need help. There must be someone out there who needs our assistance."

My eyes returned to the window. "There's no point helping Mr Mendoza with his bins. I helped him with his garden once. He gets angry if you put things in the wrong place. He's evil. His pet parrot, Brian, knows more swear words than I do."

Michael scowled. "I don't mean *him*. I mean serious help with serious problems."

"I don't think we're qualified, Michael. I haven't got my Level Three swimming certificate yet and I quit Cubs before they gave me the 'Home Help' badge."

"Rubbish," he said. "I've been trained by the Ghanaian Secret Service, remember?" (He hadn't.) "And you got that 'I Took Part' sticker at Sports Day last year." (I did.)

Outside, the rain sloshed down again. Mr Mendoza rushed indoors, his wheelie bins now spotlessly clean.

I eventually shook my head. "No, Michael. I think we should just stick to drawing. This is a ridiculous idea. There's absolutely no way that we can be superheroes. It's just not realistic. And it's dangerous. I'm going to have to put my foot down. There's no chance that I can ever ever ever agree to becoming a superhero with you."

Our costumes arrived a week later.

We'd searched for 'Jaguar' on the internet but that just gave us posh cars for rich people. We changed it to 'Jaguar Superhero Costume' but still couldn't find anything suitable. In the end, Mum bought me a cheetah onesie from a very very very very very expensive shop called Primark. The costume was a bit baggy and the round ears on top were a bit like Mickey Mouse ears – only with spots on.  But once I'd attached my cape (a black towel from the airing cupboard), it looked like the real deal.

Michael was less impressed with his mandrill outfit.

"It doesn't fit me!" he complained.

He'd bought a Rafiki costume (you know, the ape from The Lion King).  It was two sizes too small because that's all they had at the Disney Store.  Michael managed to squeeze his limbs into the tiny outfit but it was practically bursting at the seams.

"It's skin-tight," I reassured him.  "That's how superheroes are *supposed* to wear them.  Black Panther, Batman, Jane Fonda."

"Who?"

"Black Panther.  His costume is really tight.  You'll look just like him."

Okay, so this may have been a white lie.  He didn't look good.  Along with the tight-fit, Michael also had huge tufts of white fur surrounding his face, giving him a Santa vibe.  And to top it off, the red and blue face had a huge cartoon smile, nothing like a tough superhero, though I didn't mention this to Michael.

I attached a cape (blue towel from the airing cupboard) to Michael's outfit, which cheered him slightly.

"You two look cool," my mum stated, when we sat down for Saturday night pizza. "But you know it's not Halloween for another six weeks, don't you?"

"We're just getting inspiration," I replied, "for our comics." I winked at Michael and we gently bumped elbows (which we did instead of a fist-bump).

"What are you doing tonight?" Mum asked.

"Nothing much," I lied. "Just working on our comic. We'll stay out of your way. We probably won't even leave my room."

We snuck out the house at 6pm.

We aimed to be home for eight, giving us two whole hours to save lives and be generally super. After dinner, Michael made a sign for my bedroom door:

**Doo Not Disterb! Geeniuses at Wurk!**

Hopefully, it would keep Mum out.

We crept through the shadows to the end of our road, turned the corner and darted into the nearby woods. Our superhero HQ was hidden in the middle of the trees, between two thick bushes. It had a log in the centre, a sheet of tarpaulin overhead and a stick by the entrance. The stick used to have a flag attached to it, with **JJ + MM HQ** written in felt tip. But we'd made the flag from paper and, at the first sign of rain, it had disintegrated.

"So who exactly are we going to help?" I asked, as we sat beneath the tarpaulin, the pleasant September air keeping us warm.

Michael, with his red and blue face and great tufts of white hanging around his neck, simply shrugged. "Maybe an old lady needs help crossing the road. Or a cat might be stuck in a tree."

I sighed. "I thought you wanted to do serious help with serious problems? That sounds like being back at Cubs."

Michael nodded. "Let's go to Foster Park. Anything could be happening down there."

With that, Michael stood up, stepped out of our headquarters and sprinted off through the woods, his blue cape and bits of white beard trailing behind him. I quickly followed. Like

Batman and Robin, we stuck to the shadows of every street, all the way to the park. We only saw one person on our way down there; Mrs Fretwell walking her poodle, Sheila, along Cumberland Avenue. But we managed to duck behind an old Fiat Punto without her spotting us.

Foster Park was a big, open space with a huge swan-friendly pond in the centre. There were plenty of trees and shadowy areas for us to stay hidden. Not that we needed to. There was no one around... at first.

We were about to go and look at the ducks on the pond when we suddenly heard voices. We shuffled back into the shadows and watched as Dylan Tarr, a twelve-year-old with a bad reputation, strutted along the footpath with a friend from the secondary school. They were both wearing tracksuits and baseball caps. And... they were smoking!

Knots suddenly twisted in my stomach. Dylan was a nasty kid from a nasty family. Last year, his teacher had tied her hair into a ponytail. Dylan picked up a pair of scissors, snuck behind her and chopped the ponytail clean off! When our headteacher, Miss Frearson, called Dylan's mum to suspend him, the whole family came to the school office, furious. They blamed the teacher for having scissors in the classroom and refused to take Dylan out of class.

Worst of all, Dylan lived on my street, next door to Mr Mendoza. I dreaded being seen by him… especially dressed like this!

"This is our chance," Michael whispered.

I scowled. "Our chance to do what?"

"To be superheroes. We could do something about this."

"About what?" I hissed. "They're not doing anything?"

"They're smoking!"

"So what?"

Michael huffed. "Jeremy, they're only a year older than us."

"You said that being a superhero was about saving people. Who would we be saving?"

"We could save Dylan… from nicotine! He might listen to a superhero."

*Yes,* I thought, *but not two characters who look like Jungle Book rejects.*

A sickly feeling suddenly churned in my guts. Something was wrong. The park had gone quiet. Dylan and his friend had stopped walking. Out the corner of my eye, I saw them looking in our direction. My heart turned to ice.

"Oi!" yelled Dylan. "Who's there?"

Michael and I froze, barely daring to breathe.

"Who is it?" Dylan shouted. His friend said a horrible swear word. Dylan bent down to the footpath, picked up a rock and flung it in our direction. Missing us by less than a metre, the rock crashed into the undergrowth, cracking branches. We somehow managed not to scream or duck or even move at all. Dylan and his friend cackled at their mini act of destruction before swaggering off through the park. Dylan's friend repeated his swear word at the top of his voice. We watched them strut away, clouds of smoke billowing above their heads.

"That went well," I said, turning to Michael. "And that was without them even seeing us."

"Look, if you're just going to be negative, we might as well go home."

"I'm not trying to be negative. I just don't think that Dylan Tarr and his family of criminals should be who we target to help. It should be someone innocent, someone helpless, someone who has no choice about their situation. You know, like the friendly dragon in our comic, kidnapped by the old wizard and put into a cage."

Michael laughed. "Yeah but we're not going to find someone trapped in a cage around here, are we?" He paused for a moment before his face lit up. "Actually, you might be onto something, Jeremy. What did you once say about that guy who lives on your street?"

I frowned, struggling to remember. "Niall O'Leary? The bloke who married his car?"

Michael shook his head. "No, not him. The guy across the road. The one with the bins."

"Mr Mendoza? What, you think he's got someone trapped inside his wheelie bin? I doubt it."

"No. You said he had a parrot or something. Ryan?"

I nodded. "Yes. Brian."

"Well, how horrible is that?"

I shrugged. "I don't know. How horrible is it?"

"It's disgusting. You have a big, beautiful bird like that. A tropical bird that's used to flying around South American jungles or Caribbean beaches, free to go wherever it wants. And you stick it in a tiny cage, with nowhere to go, no other birds to play with, no chance to spread its colourful wings and soar through the air. This is our calling, Jeremy. This is the mission for Michael Mandrill and Jeremy Jaguar. We need to set that bird free! And other birds too!" His voice sparkled with excitement. "Birds around the country are caged up against their free will, just like the dragon in our story. This is our chance. Our chance to be superheroes!"

I frowned. Everything he said sounded right. No, not just right... righteous. But at the same time, it felt wrong.

"I'm not so sure," I eventually said. "So, we break into Mr Mendoza's house, open his parrot's cage and just let it loose... without him noticing?"

"It's the right thing to do, Jeremy. Think of poor Brian, stuck inside that tight space with nowhere to go and nothing to do but listen to that grumpy git all day."

"But Mr Mendoza will kill us if he sees us. You've not seen the rage in his eyes when you put his watering can in the shed instead of the greenhouse. Imagine what he'd do if he caught us releasing his parrot. He'd have our guts for garters!"

Michael's face screwed up. "What does that mean?"

"I've got no idea. Mum says it." I paused, choosing my next words carefully. "Look, I can see your point and everything and I think it's an honourable idea to free exotic birds. But we can't go breaking into people's houses and setting their pets loose. There's no way I can agree to this. It's just not realistic. And it's dangerous. I'm going to have to put my foot down. There's no chance that I'm ever ever ever ever ever going to break into Mr Mendoza's house with you."

Five minutes later, we were standing outside Mr Mendoza's house; Michael in his tight bearded-ape costume, me looking like a packet of Cheetos. Next door, at Dylan Tarr's house, voices could be heard through the walls; deep gorilla-like grunts, followed by shrieking cackles. Dylan's parents, boozing cheap cider at home, like every Saturday night.

*No wonder Mr Mendoza's so grumpy all the time!*

"I still think we should stick to drawing the superheroes," I muttered.

"Just relax," said Michael. "We're freeing someone who's innocent, helpless, someone who has no choice about their situation. Just like you said."

I sighed dramatically. "So what am I supposed to say?"

"Just tell him that you saw someone tampering with his bins. That'll get his knickers in a twist."

"But that's a lie," I said.

Michael frowned. "You told Mr Hopton that your snails ate your homework last week. Anyway, on my way around the back, I'll put something in his bin, then it won't be a lie."

"So, you're going to walk right in the back door?"

Michael nodded. "Yes."

"What if it's locked?"

Michael lifted his hands as if to feel the air. "Jeremy, it's September. It's warm. He's bound to have a window open or something. It'll be fine. Just keep him talking until I've released Brian."

Michael darted across the street.

"Wait!" I said. "Be careful. Their back doors are right next to each other. Do *not* go in the red door."

Michael didn't stop to look back. He just waved his hand. "Yeah, yeah. Red door. Got it," he said, before disappearing into the shadows at the side of Mr Mendoza's house. I took a deep breath, swallowed hard and then tottered hesitantly across

the road.  Pausing before the front door, I straightened my
superhero costume before ringing the bell.

*PING.  PONG.*

More cackles of laughter erupted next door.  I'd never realised
that Dylan's dad could be so funny.  He didn't seem capable of
completing full sentences in my experience, never mind stand-
up comedy.

I tapped my fingers against my thigh as I waited nervously.
For a moment, I thought that Mr Mendoza wasn't home so we
could forget all about this silly stunt.  But then I heard someone
shuffling around inside the house.

The door creaked open slightly.  Mr Mendoza had a chain
attached to the handle so that no one could force their way in.
His face appeared in the gap.  It was wrinkled, leathery and the
colour of caramel.

"Jeremy Green?" he said, his voice raspy and cold.  "What do
you want?  Do you know what time it is?  Why are you dressed
like Tony the Tiger?"

"Well, actually, a cheetah.  I'm meant to be a jaguar but they
didn't have any jaguar cost–"

"What do you want?" Mr Mendoza barked. "There's a classic episode of *Time Team* on the telly and I don't want to miss it."

Butterflies fluttered in my tummy. "Well, erm, it's just–"

"Spit it out!"

"I saw someone messing with your bins, so I thought I'd–"

"*What?*"

Inside, the chain rattled free, before the door sprang open. Mr Mendoza charged out of his house, straight to the wheelie bins. He inspected around the sides and behind them. He looked inside and lifted each bin to check beneath. After a couple of minutes, he seemed satisfied that everything was fine.

Was Michael now inside, releasing the bird? As I watched Mr Mendoza, flustered about his bins, a pang of guilt hit me. What were we doing? Brian may be Mr Mendoza's only companion, his only friend. And we were taking that away from him. And what about the parrot himself? Would he even survive in the wilderness of Great Britain? Winter was just around the corner. Can parrots deal with low temperatures? Did they know how to emigrate? What if Brian had been in a cage all his life and didn't know how to survive in the wild?

My heart clattered in my chest. My skin became clammy. Mr Mendoza said something but I didn't hear what.

"Sorry?" I asked.

"What did the person look like? I bet it was that blummin' Dylan. What was he even doing near my bins?"

The cheetah onesie became itchy. I scratched my neck. "Well, erm –"

"Come on, boy. Spit it out! What was he doing?"

"They were just, sort of, mucking about."

"They? There was more than one? Who were they?"

"I'm not entirely sure," I said, completely making it up. "They looked kind of –"

I struggled to find the right words. My mind went blank.

But before I could think of anything to say, the sound of smashing glass erupted next door.

Someone screamed.

Dylan's mum.

"Oh my God!" she squealed. "Darren! There's a goblin in the living room!"

My heart froze. Mr Mendoza turned to look at the Tarr house. There was a bang and a thud and clatter of metal. A deep, bellowing yell came from Dylan's dad, Darren, before heavy footsteps pounded through the house.

Seconds later, Michael came galloping from the side of Mr Mendoza's house.

"Wrong house!" he squealed. "Run!"

My heart leapt into my mouth and, before I knew it, I was charging after Michael, down the street. It wasn't easy in a baggy cheetah onesie. Mr Mendoza shouted something. Then came the roar of Dylan's dad, just as we turned the corner.

"You said *red door*," said Michael, panting.

"No, I said *do not* go in the red door!"

We shot across the road, straight to the woods, zigzagging through the trees before eventually sliding into our headquarters, hidden behind the bushes and the sheet of tarpaulin.

We sat silently on our log. My knees knocked, my breathing was tight. We listened for signs that Dylan's dad had followed us... but heard nothing other than the sounds of the woods; leaves rustling in the wind, birds (or bats) flapping about. It didn't sound like we'd been followed. My stomach began to settle. My heartbeat slowed.

"I think we should just stick to drawing the superheroes," I whispered.

"I think you're right," Michael agreed, with a long sigh.

And all of a sudden, neither of us felt particularly super anymore.

# GRANDAD'S GHOST

Before moving to Thailand with his new girlfriend, my grandad lived in a scruffy terraced house, squished between its neighbouring buildings. Grandad gave up caring for the place long before he left. Empty beer cans now littered the overgrown garden and the house looked very sorry for itself, with paintwork and plaster peeling away.

Since Grandad left the country, I'd been there with Mum a few times. Her and Auntie Carol planned to sell the property and share the money between them. But the place was a mess.

Nervously twisting the key in the lock, I hesitated before grabbing the handle and pushing my way inside. The door groaned open and the house blew out an icy breath of air, goosebumps instantly kissing the skin beneath my coat. The house always felt much colder *inside* than it did outside, even in October. Like a walk-in fridge-freezer. My breath clouded like a fire-breathing dragon whenever I was in there.

Stepping onto the grim carpet, I kept my trainers on. The house smelled fusty like an old museum. As I flicked on the lights, I looked for any signs of intruders or... any*thing* else.

"Hello?" My voice echoed through the cold house.

Faded wallpaper peeled away from the damp walls, dust covered every light bulb and each corner was decorated with cobwebs. But, it appeared, I was alone.

I'd been less than impressed when Mum had asked me to fetch something from Grandad's house... on tonight of all nights!

"Jeremy, I've left a brown envelope at Grandad's," she'd said, smiling as though offering ice cream. "It's on the living room sofa. Nip over for me."

"Can't you go yourself?"

Mum scowled. "Oh, so how am I meant to make dinner *and* get things ready for the Trick-or-Treaters *and* iron your school uniform *and*..."

The Guilt Trip. Classic Mum.

I reluctantly said I'd fetch the envelope. But only if she let me eat a packet of crisps before dinner. Mum agreed, so I grabbed some Prawn Cocktail (my favourite).

And that's how I ended up here.

I hated this house. Strange things always happened, like the tapping sound that constantly rattled through the floorboards and behind the walls. Mum said it was just the old pipes but pipes didn't sound like that. And anyway, the pipes weren't even on! The place was freezing!

Yet the tapping continued.

I'd tried to work out what it could have been. Not the clock (no batteries) and not the oven (turned off at the wall). It felt like something else, some kind of… *forgotten spirit* might be lurking in the shadows, beyond my vision. I shuddered at the thought.

Another weird feature of this house: something always *moved*. And no, I don't mean Mum moving through the living room, checking the damp patches on the ceiling. I mean, something *inanimate*. Something that shouldn't move on its own.

This one time, Mum put a pen down on the kitchen worktop and when we were in the living room, minutes later, it somehow fell to the floor. *CLACK!* When it hit the laminate flooring, I almost had a heart attack! Mum had blamed the wind but all the windows had been shut. Someone, or something, had pushed that pen to the floor, I'm telling you.

And that's not the weirdest one. The last time we visited, I left my trainers by the front door, their soles flat against the floor. I probably should've kept them on, seeing as Grandad's grimy old carpets looked like they hadn't been cleaned since the seventies. Anyway, after Mum had done her inspections, she said it was time to leave. I went to put my trainers back on, only to find... both of them flipped upside down, the soles now facing the ceiling. How? How could this have happened? Unless... there was *another presence* inside the house. An invisible force with a life of its own.

I immediately spotted Mum's envelope on the sofa. I'd just picked it up when I heard a sound, a dripping noise in the kitchen. I stiffened before creeping cautiously towards it.

The kitchen stank of dirty dishwater, stale and stagnant, though no dishes had been washed there for months. A constant blob of water dripped from the tap. Had someone else been here? Mum wouldn't have left this tap dripping, would she? I put down the envelope and tried tightening the tap with one hand… but it wouldn't budge. So, placing my Prawn Cocktail crisps on the worktop, I grabbed the tap with both hands. After twisting with all my strength, the dripping eventually stopped.

Nodding in satisfaction, I felt like a real workman. A plumber. A handyman. A grown-up, capable of fixing things around the house. Chest puffed, I strutted back to the living room, ready to leave.

Then came another sound.

*Taptap-taptap-taptap-tap.*

Fast. Furious.

Remembering my surroundings, my heart quickened. I darted for the door.

Then I remembered my crisps... and the envelope. I'd left them. I rushed back to the kitchen… at which point, my blood ran cold. My nerves tightened like wires as I stared at the worktop in disbelief. The crisp packet was gone! Vanished! I looked on the floor and quickly checked the sink but the crisps were nowhere to be seen.

Someone else was here!

And they'd stolen my crisps!

My eyes flashed around the room. It felt like something was always at my vision's edge... avoiding my gaze. A ghost? An evil snack-stealing spirit?

A scream escaped my throat as I sprinted out the door (forgetting to lock it). Trick-or-Treaters glared as I charged past, almost knocking one kid to the ground.

Sprinting all the way home, my legs ached and my throat burned. And I vowed to never ever step foot in Grandad's creepy house again.

An hour later, I was standing outside Grandad's house again... now wearing a Luke Skywalker outfit. Darkness had settled into the street and the Trick-or-Treaters were now a bit taller. Fewer parents patrolled. Next to me, stood my best friend Michael, dressed as a werewolf.

"This is Michael Jackson's actual costume from the *'Thriller'* video," he told me. (It wasn't.) "It's the one he actually wore." (It wasn't.)

Also by our side, was Nazirah Hameed. She wasn't in fancy dress. Just in her usual outfit; blue dress and purple hijab. In fact, she wasn't even meant to be with us. She just bumped into us on her way to the shop.

"Haunted, you say?" I could tell she was intrigued because she nodded her head and then said: "I'm intrigued. Can I come with you?" Nazirah was super smart, like a professor or a calculator or the woman who does the maths on *Countdown*.

"We're not hanging around," I said. "I left an envelope in there, so I just need to grab it. Then we leave."

I pushed open the door. Inside, the chill immediately hit my bones once more. Our breaths clouded the air.

"Woooooah," said Michael, inspecting Grandad's flowery curtains. "These definitely look haunted. Shame I didn't bring my ghost-detecting machine."

(Michael didn't have a ghost-detecting machine.)

Grabbing the envelope from the sofa, I turned for the exit but Nazirah was already in the kitchen.

"Hey! Wait! We're not hanging around," I shouted, tossing the envelope back down.

"So, your crisps vanished here?" asked Nazirah. Michael and I stepped through.

"Yes," I said. "Prawn Cocktail. I left them just there, next to the sink. Now, come on, let's go."

"Hang on," said Nazirah. "Maybe we can get to the bottom of this. There's usually a simple explanation for paranormal activity, a logical explanation. This kind of thing is usually all in a person's head. If someone is told that a place is haunted, they're more likely to see strange shapes or hear odd noises or... think something has moved, even when it hasn't."

I laughed. "So, you're saying I imagined it? Oh, well, thanks for clearing that one up, Doctor Hameed. I guess I'm just a nutcase."

Nazirah shook her head. "No, I'm not saying you're going crazy or anything. Maybe you just *misremembered* where you'd put the crisps. You thought they were in the kitchen but... they weren't. Your belief that this place is haunted kicks in and, well, you think a ghost has stolen them, rather than doing the logical thing and looking elsewhere."

I grunted. "I know where I left them, Nazirah."

"Look, scientists carried out a study where they gave tours of an old theatre to different groups. Some groups were told that the theatre was haunted, other groups were not. Guess which groups always claimed they'd experienced paranormal activity? Strange noises, movement behind them, the feeling of another, unseen presence."

I frowned. "What's this got to do with my crisps?"

"It was the groups who'd been told that the theatre was haunted. And do you know how many people in the other groups sensed paranormal goings-on? None." She folded her arms. "There must be an explanation for these vanishing crisps. Ghosts aren't real, Jeremy."

"Ghosts *are* real," said Michael. "I've seen forty-three."

"No, you haven't," said Nazirah.

"Yes, I have. I've seen the ghost of Prince Harry."

"Prince Harry's not even dead."

Michael frowned. "Oh. Well, who's that other one? Kanye West?"

"He looks nothing like Prince Harry," I said. "How'd you get those two mixed up?"

"He's not dead either," said Nazirah.

The noise then started behind the walls.

*Taptap-taptap-taptap-tap.*

"What's that?" asked Michael.

"That's the tapping I told you about," I said. I turned to Nazirah. "If it's all in my head, how come you can hear it too?"

Everyone fell silent as we listened.

*Taptap-taptap-taptap-tap.*

"What is it?" asked Michael, before charging out of the kitchen and up the creaking staircase.

"Wait! No!" But it was too late. Michael had gone. I hated the upstairs at Grandad's even more than downstairs. It had felt derelict when he lived here. Now it was even worse.

"Okay," said Nazirah. "So you left your crisps here. And then what?" She dragged a finger across the grimy worktop.

I rubbed my hands to warm them. "I went into the living room, came back in here and they'd vanished. I only left them for –"

A shout from upstairs suddenly stopped me.

"Guys!" Michael yelled. "You need to see this."

With my heart thrashing in my chest, I charged to the upper floor, taking the steps two at a time. Michael stood at the doorway to Grandad's old bedroom. He was staring into the room with a worried expression on his face. I heard Nazirah come up behind me. As we peered into the room, my pulse thudded in my throat. I couldn't believe my eyes. Surely this wasn't real.

The room was plain and simple. Brown carpet, beige wallpaper and an ancient wardrobe. Dark curtains, a framed painting of a boat on the wall and, of course, a bed. And the bed was the point of our focus. The point of our fear.

On the edge of Grandad's bed, sat an antique porcelain doll, with a hard shiny face, cold blue eyes and an unsmiling mouth. An icy tickle of fear stroked the back of my neck. Had it been there when I last came with Mum? I couldn't remember seeing it before… ever.

Even more worrying than that, however, lay on the floor… right beneath the doll's feet. A packet of Prawn Cocktail crisps had been ripped open, its contents scattered on the carpet. Knots twisted in my stomach, my breathing tightened and then Nazirah said: "Oh, come on, Jeremy. You're gonna have to do better than that."

Michael laughed. "Yeah, great prank, Jez. Nice try."

"What? No! This is nothing to do with me! I left the crisps in the kitchen. Then they vanished. I've never seen that doll before in my life... I don't think."

Michael frowned.

Nazirah raised a dubious eyebrow, before saying: "So, you expect us to believe that this... *creepy* doll stole your crisps while you weren't looking, brought them up here and starting eating them?"

"I've never seen that doll before."

Michael continued to frown. "Actually... I saw its eyes move before you two came upstairs."

Now I was dubious. Anything Michael claimed to be true probably wasn't.

"So if you've never seen it before," said Nazirah, "where has it come from? And why are your crisps by its feet?"

A lump hardened in my throat. "I don't know."

"Maybe it's possessed," said Michael. "Maybe it contains your grandad's spirit."

I tutted. "My grandad isn't dead. He just moved to Thailand with his girlfriend."

"Should we touch it?" asked Nazirah. "Perhaps it says where it's from, underneath the clothing."

"I'm not looking up its skirt!" said Michael.

I wanted to laugh but couldn't. The creeping sense of dread that something otherworldly haunted the shadows of this crumbling house stopped me from even smiling.

A moment of tense silence passed as we gazed at the shiny-faced doll. Its cold blue eyes stared right back into ours, as if it could read the thoughts at the back of our brains.

"I hate it," I eventually stated. "Maybe we should destroy it. Bonfire night next week. We could use it as a Guy Fawkes."

"It might be cursed," said Michael. "If you did that, it might haunt you forever."

"Yeah," Nazirah sarcastically added. "You might never be able to eat crisps in peace again."

The tapping started again in another room.

*Taptap-taptap-taptap-tap.*

We all turned to look behind us at a closed door, its red paint faded and flaky.

"What's in there?" asked Nazirah.

"That's the bathroom," I said.

Michael took a step towards it. "Well, if the tapping is coming from there then it ain't the doll, is it?"

I glanced nervously at the creepy porcelain figure on the bed. I felt sure that I'd never seen it before. But maybe I had. Maybe I'd found the doll so disturbing that I'd just blanked it from my mind, pushed it way back, away from the nice memories, into the deepest, darkest corner of my brain, never to be thought about again.

*Taptap-taptap-taptap-tap.*

"Perhaps it's a spider," I suggested, glancing at the cobwebs in the corner.

"A spider?" said Nazirah. "What's it wearing? Tap-dancing shoes?"

She had a good point. There may have been a bucket-load of spiders in the house but they were always pretty silent. I can't remember ever being woken up by a noisy spider in the middle of the night.

"I've seen a spider wearing shoes before," said Michael.

We ignored him as we stepped closer to the bathroom. The tapping continued. Michael pressed a nervous hand on the red door. It creaked open. As we peered into the room, I was suddenly struck by how ramshackle the place looked. Floor tiles were cracked and grimy. A medicine cabinet had a mirror on its doors – with glass so dirty you couldn't see a clear reflection.

There was a huge chip missing from the corner of the sink, as if someone had smacked it with a hammer. And the toilet seat was missing from the loo.

Is this how Grandad had left it? Had he really lived in this… *squalor*? We could practically taste the stench of stale urine that hung in the air.

Yet, despite everything, one item drew our attention… the bath. Right now, we couldn't see into the tub because a filthy shower curtain had been drawn around it. The grimy curtain was supposed to be white, I think, but was now a grubby shade of yellowing grey with brown mould patches clinging to the bottom.

Was the curtain drawn the last time I was here? Did I even come into this room? I couldn't remember. A sense of unease twisted in my gut. Why would the curtain be drawn? What was it hiding?

*Taptap-taptap-taptap-tap.*

We glanced at each other nervously. The tapping came from behind the curtain. Michael nodded at me to move forwards. I shook my head, before pointing at Nazirah. She folded her arms in refusal. We stood in silence for a moment, none of us daring to move.

*Taptap-taptap-taptap-tap.*

I felt a hand in my back. And before I could protest, Michael had shoved me forward towards the bath. I scowled back at him before turning to face the dirty curtain. The tapping had momentarily stopped. I pulled the Lightsaber from my Luke Skywalker belt and held it in one hand. Ready for action, ready to defend myself. The Lightsaber was only a blue tube made of plastic so I'm not entirely sure how much use it would have been against an evil crisp-stealing spirit.

Anyway, placing nervous fingers on the edge of the material, I filled my lungs with air and then quickly dragged the shower curtain open.

Nazirah screamed!

Michael yelled!

I flinched, jumping backwards like a reverse kangaroo… as our eyes were met by… nothing. There was nothing in the bath. Well, not exactly nothing.

Michael and Nazirah stepped forwards. We all bent over to inspect the bath and saw some tiny items scattered in the bottom of the tub.

Michael's eyes suddenly brightened. "Jackpot! Chocolate!"

In amongst the dust and the grime at the bottom of the bath, there appeared to be a smattering of tiny chocolate drops. Michael reached in and picked one up. He gave the chocolate drop a little rub on his Michael Jackson werewolf outfit before moving it to his mouth.

I tried to stop him.

"Michael, I really don't think you should –"

But it was too late. He placed the dirty treat into his mouth and started sucking and chewing. The brightness of his smile quickly changed to a grimace as his lips pursed like he'd sucked a lemon. He spat the chocolate drop onto the floor, along with a mouthful of phlegm. He continued hawking for the next thirty seconds or so. The brown colour of his face quickly drained and he looked as grey as the shower curtain.

"Told you," I said. "That chocolate was covered in filth."

"It wasn't chocolate!" Michael coughed out the words, spitting more on the floor, almost on the verge of throwing up.

"What was it then?"

Nazirah peered into the tub. "Poo," she announced.

"Poo?" I repeated. "Michael ate poo?"

Nazirah nodded. "Ironic, really. Seeing as the poo usually comes *out* of his mouth."

Michael didn't answer; he was still busy coughing his guts up. I was about to ask where the poo had come from when a *BANG* suddenly echoed from the other room. Something slamming against the floor. My chest tightened. Goosebumps pricked my skin.

"What was that?" I asked.

*Taptap-taptap-taptap-tap.* Now coming from the bedroom.

I followed Nazirah across the landing and my eyes widened when I looked at the bed. It was now empty. The doll had gone!

"It's alive!" I squealed.

"Jeremy," said Nazirah, panting, her voice a higher pitch. "What game are you playing here?"

"Me? I was in the bathroom with you. We should leave."

"This can't be real," said Nazirah. "I don't believe in ghosts or –"

*SMASH!*

The framed boat painting fell to the floor, the glass breaking, scattering across the carpet.

Nazirah screamed.

I screamed.

Nazirah ran.

I ran.

*Taptap-taptap-taptap-tap.*

Nazirah and Michael were already at the bottom of the stairs, galloping towards the front door.

I charged down after them, taking three steps at a time.

Something else banged upstairs. But I didn't turn back.

My throat was dry as I tumbled down the last few steps, before charging through the living room. I reached the front door in a matter of milliseconds and was about to leave the horrors of the cold house behind me… when I remembered the envelope. No matter what phantom – what evil spirit – may have possession of this house, it wasn't as terrifying as the thought of Mum's face if I returned empty-handed... again!

Turning to the sofa, an image of the bedroom flashed into my mind and I realised what I'd seen. As I'd left the room, I'd noticed three strange things.

Firstly, the doll, which we thought had vanished, actually lay face down on the Prawn Cocktail crisps. Not vanished, simply fallen to the floor. Secondly, in the place where the picture had hung, a big hole had appeared in the wall, as if someone had scraped their way through the plasterboards with a spoon. And thirdly, the piece of string that had held the painting on the wall had been snapped, or cut.

Someone – or some*thing* – had been playing tricks on us. Someone had pushed the doll. Someone had dug the small hole. Someone had cut the string.

What kind of presence could possibly have wanted to scare us like that? I shook my head, pushing the thoughts away. I needed to get out of the house. Grabbing the envelope from the sofa, I turned to finally run away.

And that's when another set of eyes locked into mine. I froze. The creature didn't move. It just stood there on the sofa's edge, up tall on its two hind feet. Large, pointy teeth protruded from its mouth. Dirt and dust clung to its matted, white fur. And its thick, smooth tail curled around its body like a tiny snake. The animal's shiny, button eyes were red and bright and filled with evil.

Everything suddenly made total sense. The constant tapping, the hole in the wall, the theft of the crisps, the gnawing of the string, the poo. I couldn't work out where the doll had come from. Perhaps it had been there all along. Perhaps I hadn't noticed it. Maybe this creature had put it there.

Everything added up now. This house was certainly being haunted by something... non-human. And I can honestly say that it was the biggest rat I had ever seen in my life.

Smiling to myself, I squeezed the envelope tightly in my hand. I decided not to tell the others about the rat. Nazirah might work it out eventually. But Michael would love telling everyone about my grandad's haunted house. Not haunted by a possessed doll, but by an enormous rat.

# NOTES FROM THE AUTHOR

As soon as I finished *The Curious Case of the Missing Orangutan,* I began working on my next novel, hoping to have it finished within a year. However, as the twelfth month rolled around – and I was deep into rewrite number seven (or was it eight?) – I realised that the book was going to take much longer than planned.

So, after being asked *'When is your next book coming out?'* for the 973rd time (not that I'm complaining – it's always lovely to be asked), I decided that I needed to put something out soon. I took a break from the novel and started putting together a book of short stories. I already had one done. The original draft of *You've Got Snails* was actually written after I'd finished *The Great Snail Robbery* and before *The Curious Case of the Missing Orangutan.* So, in terms of Jeremy's timeline, the events in *You've Got Snails* actually take place before *The Curious Case of the Missing Orangutan* (just in case you're interested).

So, now I had to write more stories. I immediately wanted the book to be called *Jeremy's Shorts* as it's a book of *short* stories but I also wanted one story to literally be about some shorts, so that the title had a double meaning. After struggling for an idea, I can thank my friend Sarah Weaver for losing her bikini in the wave machine at Typhoon Lagoon and providing me with the inspiration I needed for my story.

Thanks to everyone who gave me feedback on the stories; Debbie Foster, Matt Henshaw, Ste Holmes, Jen Edwards and her class at Bisley Blue Coat School in Gloucestershire, award-winning author of *The Bubble Boy* and *Check Mates* (also released this summer) Stewart Foster and anyone else who I may have forgotten (sorry).

Thanks to Dawn Roberts and everyone at Annesley Primary School for your continued support with my writing journey and thank you to all of those schools who have booked me in for author visits since 2017. You've all been awesome.

Thanks once again to Jim Rogers, who has done a wonderful job on the cover illustrations. (I'm beginning to think he can read my mind!)

A massive thank you must go to my best friend in the entire world, Charlie-Fern 'The Mother of Kittens'. I'm so grateful for your patience with me whenever I drift off into the Daydream Realm, thinking about story ideas, while you're trying to tell me a fascinating tale about social justice, pelvic floor exercises or your Top 5 Favourite Dinosaurs.

And finally, thanks also to you, the reader, for taking the time to discover more about Jeremy's world.

Happy reading!

### *Daniel Henshaw*

Oh, and here's a quick message from my kitten, Thursday, who's about to walk across the keyboard…

*Y7yhxzzzzzzzzzzzzzzzzzzzzzzzzzzzzzzzzzzzzzzzzzzzzzzzz*

*zzzzzzzzzzzzzzzzzzzzzzzzzzzz*

That's a lot of Zs. I hope it's not his review of the book!

# HAVE YOU READ DANIEL HENSHAW'S
# FIRST BOOK YET?

"A GREAT PACEY READ.
PARENTS SHOULD READ THIS BOOK AS
WELL AS KIDS. IT'S A LESSON LEARNT IN
BEING HONEST, ALL WRAPPED UP IN A
FUNNY STORY."
## WRD ABOUT BOOKS MAGAZINE

"Absolutely brilliant from start to finish!"
**Matt Peat**

"A book the whole family will read over
and over again!"
**Harley Keogh**

"Great book!
Can't wait for the next one!"
**Cyrah-Leigh Sissons**

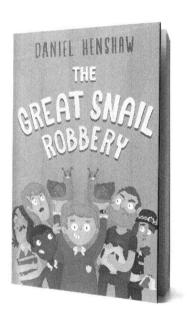

IT'S THE BOOK THAT LITERALLY ~~EVERYONE HAS BEEN~~
SOME PEOPLE HAVE BEEN TALKING ABOUT!
TURN THE PAGE TO READ THE FIRST CHAPTER.

# Chapter One:

# Death of a Goldfish

Our goldfish, Fanny, died on April 1st, three days after my tenth birthday.

I was eating burnt toast in the kitchen when Mum came in. She didn't look great. Her eyes were red, her hair was a mess and she was pulling that strange face she made when she was about to cry. She looked sadder than a turkey at Christmas. Either she had some bad news, or her hay fever was about to kick in.

"Jeremy," she said. "Fanny jumped out of your bedroom window and ended up in Mrs Patel's toolbox next door. She's dead now. Fanny, I mean. Not Mrs Patel."

I laughed at first, thinking it was an April Fool.

"Mum, you shouldn't joke about-"

Then I noticed she was actually crying and I realised that it wasn't an April Fool at all.

"Couldn't you save her?" I asked. "Did you try mouth-to-mouth?"

This sounded a lot more sensible in my head than when I said it out loud. I gave Mum a hug. It seemed a bit odd, a grown woman crying over a goldfish, but she'd been very emotional lately, with all the arguing she did with Dad.

Then I started crying too. My goldfish really was dead.

I'd always felt a bit sorry for Fanny. She must have been bored out of her mind in that empty tank. I mean, I get bored at school but at least I can look at the times-tables posters on the wall, which have funny aliens on them. Or sometimes, in the back of my book, I draw pictures of people with really long armpit hair.

What could Fanny do? Just swim around and around and around.

Still, I hadn't realised she was suicidal. So sad. Taking her dying breaths next to Mrs Patel's spanner. I'm not sure that's what Fanny would've wanted. The more I thought about it, the more I cried. And if I'd known how badly the death of a goldfish would later affect my family, I'd have somehow tried harder to save her.

Life didn't feel right without my goldfish.

**A FAMILY ISN'T COMPLETE WITHOUT A PET!**

I'd read that on a tea towel once.

\*

Following Fanny's death, spending lunchtimes at school with Miss Hope cheered me up more than anything. Miss Hope was the kindest, most caring teacher in the school, probably in the world. She had a smile that could warm-up the frostiest morning. She was the most beautiful person I'd ever seen in real life (top secret information). She had long black hair and tanned skin like an Italian. She reminded me of Pocahontas from the Disney film.

Miss Hope let me stay in at lunchtimes because I helped to look after our class pets. Nobody else was interested in them. Just me.

"They disgucking," Leah Ford had said (she can't talk properly).

"They're dead boring," said Alfie Brown. "They're more boring than wallpaper… or radiators… or moss."

Everyone wanted hamsters or guinea pigs or even rats. Instead, we had two Giant African Land Snails… and I loved them!

Miss Hope had named them Pea and Pod because, when they were first born, they were smaller than her finger nail. Now they're bigger than both my hands put together. And I was the only person in class who dared pick them up. Even my best friend Michael didn't like touching them and his family are from Africa, just like the snails.

It was a Thursday lunchtime — just over a week since Fanny died — when Miss Hope said something that stuck in my brain like PVA glue.

Class was empty. Peaceful and quiet. Pod was greedily sucking on some cucumber, Pea was sliming his way across my hands and then Miss Hope gave me one of those smiles that made my heart skip.

"You must be filled with kindness, Jeremy," she said. "Because looking after animals fills your heart with kindness and love."

A tingle ran down my neck. *Miss Hope thought I was filled with kindness and love.* A warm glow surged through my body. Miss Hope always knew the right words to cheer me up. And later that evening I would remember her words so clearly, because that Thursday would soon become the worst day of my ten years on Earth.

\*

My life began to fall apart while I was sitting at the kitchen table, eating alphabet spaghetti and watching Countdown. I'm not very good at Countdown but I *do* like the clock music.

Then Mum came in. Black make-up tears ran down her face, so I knew something was up.

"Jeremy," she said, sniffling. "I need you to sit down for a minute."

"I am sitting down," I said.

She picked up the remote and turned off the TV, which was annoying because I'd just found a five-letter word — my best score ever. I didn't complain though because I could see Mum was upset. And what she said next made everything go swirly. I think I nearly fainted but I can't properly remember.

"Your dad and I are getting a divorce. He's moved out already and is buying a house on the other side of town. You'll still see him at weekends."

My throat felt sore and my lips started to quiver as I tried not to cry. I had to stop myself from being sick.

None of it made sense. Mum and Dad loved each other. They always had and they always would... until the end of time... that's what I'd thought anyway.

So, what had changed?

Upstairs, I found Dad's wardrobe empty.

It was true. He'd gone.

I couldn't stop the crying now. Tears drenched my face and snot dripped from my nose. I told Mum that I hated her. This was all her fault.

"Dad wouldn't leave unless you made him!" I screamed. I called her a cow and a pig and other animals too.

"You're just a... stupid otter!"

Not sure where that one came from.

I sobbed into my bed sheets for a long, long time.

Then I gazed out of the window for ages, just staring at trees and walls and fences. Wishing, hoping, praying that this was all a bad dream and I'd soon wake up.

I pinched myself. That's what people on telly do to wake themselves up if they think they're in a dream.

I didn't wake up.

Staring at Mrs Patel's fence next door, I was reminded of Fanny's final flight, over the fence and into the toolbox. My poor little pet.

And then a thought hit me. An idea began bubbling in my mind. I thought about the way that things had altered over the past week or so. And then it became clear in my head, like a vision. I could see the problem solving itself in my mind. I knew exactly how to get Dad back to our house... so that we could be a proper family again.

 Daniel Henshaw is the author of **'The Great Snail Robbery'**, **'The Curious Case of the Missing Orangutan'** and **'Jeremy's Shorts'**, all starring Jeremy Green. One of Daniel's stories has been shortlisted for the **'Best Novel for Children'** at the Wells Festival of Literature. His short stories have been published in magazines and online literary publications.

Daniel is a qualified primary school teacher with a degree in English Studies. He loves football. His favourite teams are Notts County and Selston FC.

He lives in Derbyshire with his girlfriend and two kittens.

**Follow Daniel on Twitter: @AuthorHenshaw**

**Or keep up-to-date with Jeremy Green at:**

**Facebook.com/JeremySnails**

# DANIEL HENSHAW

## AUTHOR DAY & KS2 MYSTERY WRITING WORKSHOPS

**Daniel also visits schools! Most recently he's been to...**

**London**: Gordon Primary;  **Liverpool**: Springwood Heath Primary;

**Cheshire**: Adswood Primary;  **Northamptonshire**: Beanfield Primary,

Oakley Vale Primary;  **Nottinghamshire**: Annesley Primary, Morven Park

Primary, Dalestorth Primary, Robert Mellors Primary, Wainwright Primary,

Samuel Barlow Primary, Hawthorne Primary, Mount Primary; Brinsley

Primary;  **Derbyshire**: Tansley Primary, Loscoe Primary, Horsley

Woodhouse Primary, Coppice Primary, Wirksworth Junior, Ashbourne

Hilltop

---

"Daniel's whole school assembly was exciting and funny. He did

exactly what we had hoped, capturing the children's imagination

and really inspiring them for a day of writing mystery stories."

Robert Mellors Primary School, Arnold, Nottingham

---

If you're interested in this opportunity, email:

**mrdhenshaw@gmail.com** for details.

Printed in Poland
by Amazon Fulfillment
Poland Sp. z o.o., Wrocław